WHERE IS CHICKEN POX?

by Tracey West

Based on
"THE POWERPUFF GIRLS,"
as created by Craig McCracken

SCHOLASTIC INC.

New York   Toronto   London   Auckland   Sydney
Mexico City   New Delhi   Hong Kong   Buenos Aires

ISBN 0-439-29587-4

Designed by Peter Koblish
Illustrated by The Thompson Brothers

12 11 10 9 8 7 6 5 4 3 2   1 2 3 4 5 6/0

Printed in the U.S.A.

First Scholastic printing, September 2001

The city of Townsville! It was another busy day for The Powerpuff Girls.

Smashing monsters is hard work. Blossom, Bubbles, and Buttercup went right to bed. But something happened while they were asleep. Something very strange . . .

The next morning, the Girls woke up. They looked at one another.

"Gross! There are red bumps all over you," yelled Buttercup.

"They are all over you, too," Blossom said back.

"I am itchy," Bubbles said.

"I think a bad guy did this to us," Blossom said. "He got us when we were asleep."

Buttercup flew out of bed. "Let's get him!"

The Girls went into the kitchen. Professor Utonium was on the phone. He was talking to their teacher, Ms. Keane.

"The Girls will not be coming to school today," he said. "Chicken Pox has got them!"

"I knew it!" Blossom said. "Chicken Pox must be a bad guy."

"We should find him before he can do this to anyone else," said Bubbles.

Buttercup did not want to wait. "Let's go!" she yelled.

"Let's go see Mojo Jojo," said Blossom. "I bet that evil monkey knows where Chicken Pox is."
The Girls flew to Mojo Jojo's place.

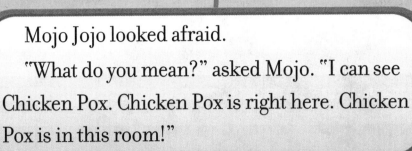

Mojo Jojo looked afraid.

"What do you mean?" asked Mojo. "I can see Chicken Pox. Chicken Pox is right here. Chicken Pox is in this room!"

The Powerpuff Girls looked behind them. They did not see Chicken Pox anywhere.

"He got away!" Bubbles wailed.

"This Chicken Pox guy is pretty smart," said Blossom. "I hope we find him soon. I feel itchy all over!"

"Let's go see Fuzzy Lumpkins," said Bubbles.
"Maybe he knows where Chicken Pox is."
The Girls flew to Fuzzy's house.

"Where is Chicken Pox?" they asked Fuzzy Lumpkins.

Fuzzy hid behind his chair.

"Do not bring Chicken Pox into this here house!" he said.

The Powerpuff Girls looked behind them. Chicken Pox must have followed them!

"Chicken Pox must be really fast," said Bubbles. "I hope we catch him soon. I feel itchy all over!"

"Let's try the Gangreen Gang next," said Buttercup. "I bet those gross green goofs know where to find Chicken Pox."

The Girls flew to the Gangreen Gang's hideout.

"Where is Chicken Pox?" they asked the Gang.

The Gang hid in a closet. "We do not want any Chicken Pox here!" yelled Ace, their leader.

"Chicken Pox must be really tough," said Buttercup. "All the bad guys are afraid of him."

"We have to find him," Blossom said.

The Girls flew to Pokey Oaks Kindergarten.

Blossom knocked on the window.

"Ms. Keane, have you seen Chicken Pox?" Blossom asked her teacher.

Ms. Keane would not let them inside. "You Girls cannot come in here with Chicken Pox," she said.

The Powerpuff Girls looked behind them.

"Chicken Pox followed us again!" said Buttercup. "He must be a real chicken. He keeps running away from us."

"Maybe he is not chicken," said Bubbles. "Maybe he is trying to trick us. He will not let us catch him."

"This is big," said Blossom. "We need to warn the Mayor."

The Girls flew to Townsville City Hall.

"Mayor, we need to tell you something," the Girls said.

The Mayor smiled. "Oh, I see you Girls have Chicken Pox," he said.

The Girls looked behind them. Chicken Pox must have followed them again! But they could not see him anywhere.

"I got Chicken Pox when I was a little boy," said the Mayor.

"You did?" asked Blossom. "Tell us about it! We need to find out all we can about Chicken Pox."

The Mayor leaned back in his chair. "I was just a little lad. . . ." he began.

The Mayor talked and talked. The Girls listened. But they felt tired. And itchy. And warm.

Ms. Bellum came to the rescue. "Let me take you Girls home," she said.

Soon they were home. Professor Utonium tucked them into bed.

"But we have to stop Chicken Pox," said Blossom.

"He is a bad guy," said Bubbles.

"He did this to us," said Buttercup.

Professor Utonium smiled. "Oh, Girls. Chicken Pox is not a person. You are sick. Many kids get chicken pox. You will feel better soon."

The Powerpuff Girls fell asleep.

That night, something happened to Mojo Jojo, Fuzzy Lumpkins, and the Gangreen Gang. Red bumps popped up on their skin. They felt itchy all over. "We have chicken pox!" they wailed.

So once again, the day was saved . . . thanks to Professor Utonium and a good night's sleep!